SEE ME DIG

Leschi Elementary School
135 32nd. Avenue
Seattle, WA. 98122

SEE ME DIG

by Paul Meisel

I Like to Read®

HOLIDAY HOUSE • NEW YORK

For Cheryl.
And for Rusty, our blind Brittany spaniel,
who likes to dig.

I LIKE TO READ is a registered trademark of Holiday House Publishing, Inc.

Copyright © 2013 by Paul Meisel
All Rights Reserved
HOLIDAY HOUSE is registered in the U.S. Patent and Trademark Office.
Printed and Bound in April 2017 at Tien Wah Press, Johor Bahru, Johor, Malaysia.
The artwork was executed in pen and ink, acrylic, pencil,
and watercolor on Waterford watercolor paper.
www.holidayhouse.com
5 7 9 10 8 6

Library of Congress Cataloging-in-Publication Data
Meisel, Paul.
See me dig / by Paul Meisel. — 1st ed.
p. cm. — (I like to read)
Companion book to See me run.
Summary: A group of dogs that loves to dig has a fun-filled day
of making mischief in this easy-to-read story.
ISBN 978-0-8234-2743-7 (hardcover)
[1. Dogs—Fiction.] I. Title.
PZ7.M5158752Sdm 2013
[E]—dc23
2012016549

ISBN 978-0-8234-3057-4 (paperback)
GRL D

See me dig.
I like to dig.

We all like to dig.
We dig and dig.

Oh, no! They are mad.

We run away.

We can dig here.

What is this?

It is a box.

We tug and tug and tug.

Oh, no!
They are mad.

We run and run.

We must stop them.
I will be brave.

Woof!

Woof! Woof!
See them go.
I am a hero.

He likes to dig too.

Now we dig some more!

I Like to Read® Books
You will like all of them!

Paperback and Hardcover

Boy, Bird, and Dog by David McPhail

Dinosaurs Don't, Dinosaurs Do by Steve Björkman

Fish Had a Wish by Michael Garland

I Will Try by Marilyn Janovitz

Late Nate in a Race by Emily Arnold McCully

The Lion and the Mice
by Rebecca Emberley and Ed Emberley

See Me Run by Paul Meisel
A Theodor Seuss Geisel Award Honor Book

Hardcover

Car Goes Far by Michael Garland

The Fly Flew In by David Catrow

I Have a Garden by Bob Barner

Look! by Ted Lewin

Mice on Ice
by Rebecca Emberley and Ed Emberley

Pig Has a Plan by Ethan Long

Sam and the Big Kids by Emily Arnold McCully

Sick Day by David McPhail

You Can Do It! by Betsy Lewin

Visit holidayhouse.com to read more
about I Like to Read® Books.

I Like to Read® Books in Paperback
You will like all of them!

Visit http://www.holidayhouse.com/I-Like-to-Read/ for more about I Like to Read® books, including flash cards, reproducibles, and the complete list of titles.